Lucy Visit
the
SUPER Market

story by:
ashlie hammond

pictures by:
robin robinson

Lucy Visits the SUPER Market

First Edition

No portion of this publication may be reproduced (except for review purposes) by any means without express written permission from Monkey Minion Press or an agent of Monkey Minion Press.

ISBN-13: 978-1478120919
ISBN-10: 1478120916

To all of our nieces & nephews
- may your errands never
lose that chance for adventure.

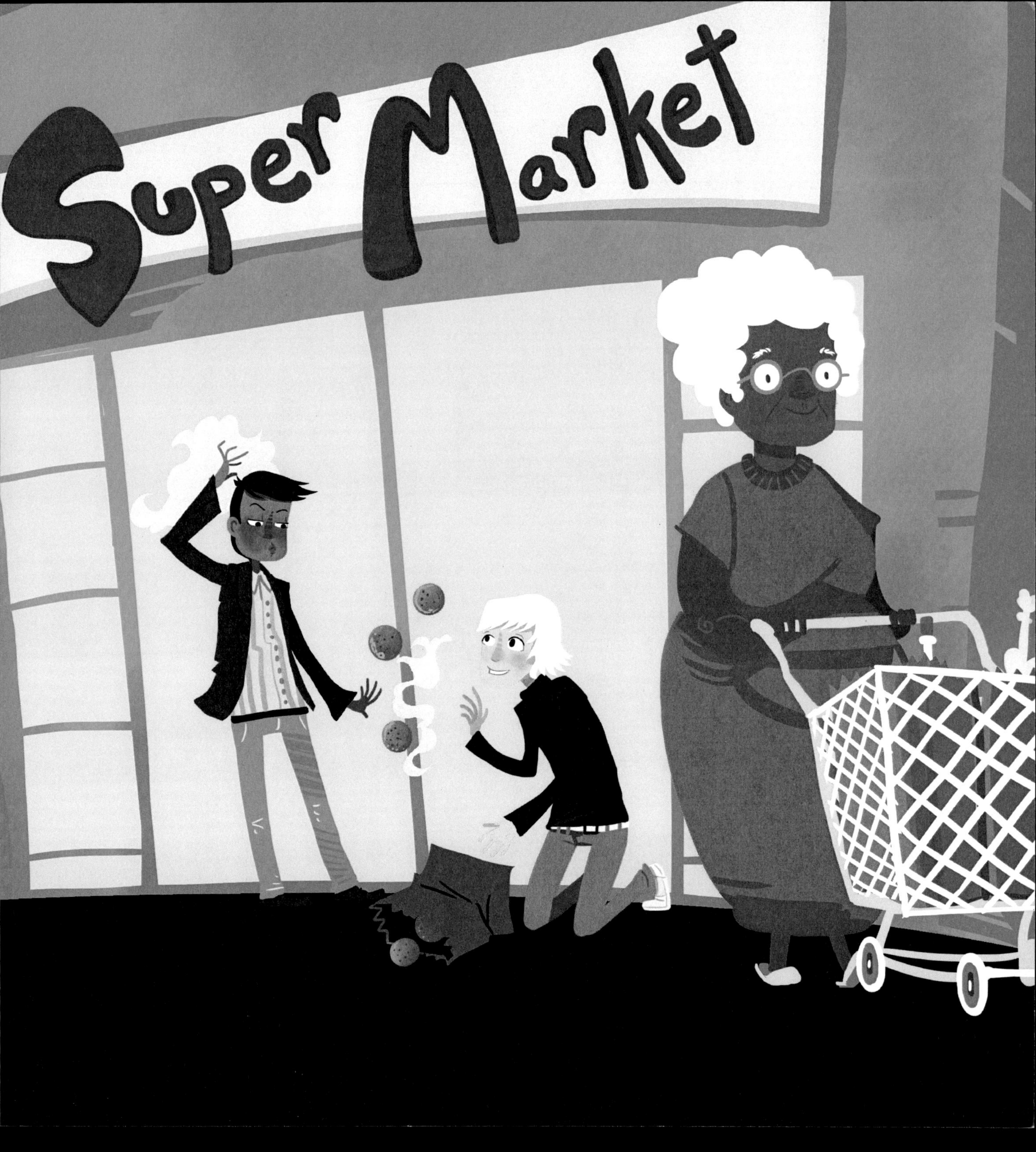
Super Market

TRY ME!

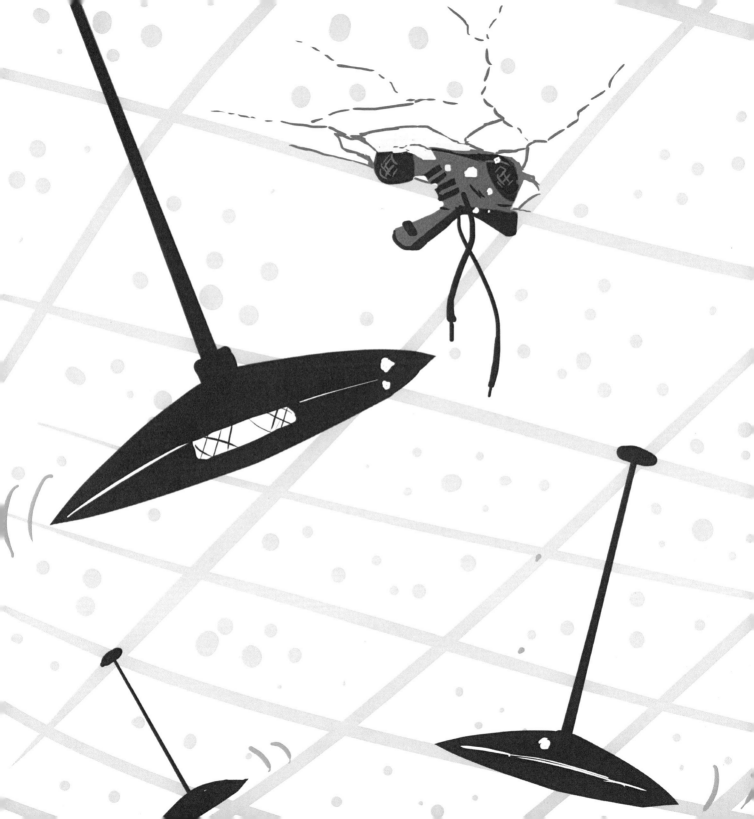

The End.

31377045R00022

Made in the USA
San Bernardino, CA
08 March 2016